characters created by lauren child

# I want to be much more bigger like you

PUFFIN

Text based on the script written by Carol Noble

Illustrations from the TV animation produced by Tiger Aspect

PUFFIN BOOKS
Published by the Penguin Group: London, New York, Australia,
Canada, India, Ireland, New Zealand and South Africa
Penguin Books Ltd, Registered Offices: 80 Strand, London WC2R 0RL, England

puffinbooks.com

This edition published in Great Britain in Puffin Books 2010
1 3 5 7 9 8 6 4 2
Text and illustrations copyright © Lauren Child / Tiger Aspect Productions Limited, 2008
The Charlie and Lola Logo is a trademark of Lauren Child
All rights reserved. The moral right of the author/illustrator has been asserted
Manufactured in China
ISBN: 978-0-141-33497-4
This edition produced for The Book People Ltd,
Hall Wood Avenue, Haydock, St Helens, WA11 9UL

I have this little sister Lola.
She is small and very funny.
Lola says, "I'm not small, Charlie.
I am getting more **bigger**
and grown-up all of the time."

"And now that I am
much more **bigger**,
I can go on the
**Super-Duper
Loopy Loopy** ride."

So I say,
"The **Super-Duper
Loop the Looper** is
very, **very SCARY.**
Are you sure?"

"I am **very** sure, Charlie,"
says Lola.

So I measure Lola
to see if she really is
bigger.

"Charlie, I must be
more taller than that!
Are you tricking me?"

"No, Lola. That's exactly
how big you are."

Then Lola says,
"But, I absolutely MUST
be big enough to
go on the Super-Duper
Loopy Loopy ride."

I say, "There are still
loads of **fun rides**
          at the fair for
smaller people.
          The **Chug-a-Bugs**
ride is really exciting."


And Lola says,
"I don't think so, Charlie."

Then Lola says,
"I have a GOOD plan.
I am going to
think myself bigger.

Now I am thinking
I am nearly as
big as a sunflower
touching the sun...

"And now I am thinking I am as **big** as one of those extremely

T
A
L
L
E
S
T

buildings."

I say,
"You can't MAKE yourself
**bigger**, Lola.
It just happens."

Lola says,
        "It's not fair.
Why am I always, always
        the small one?"

So I say,
        "There are great
things about
        being small. Like...

" ... you get **stories**
read to you
every night...

and you get loads of
**piggybacks.**"

But Lola says,
"I still really, **really**
would like being
the **biggest.**"

When Marv comes over,
he says,
"Are you ready for
the **Super-Duper**
**Loop the Looper?**"

And Lola shouts,
"I am! I am! I am!"

Then Marv whispers,
"She's quite **small** for the ride,
isn't she, Charlie?"

And I say,
"Yup."

At the fair,
Marv says,
"The **Super-Duper
Loop the Looper**
is going to be
the best ride!"

"Yes. It will make
our hair stand
on end," I say.

"And our tummies
go all **funny**,"
says Marv.
"I can't wait!
How about you, Lola?"

"Err... I can't wait either..."

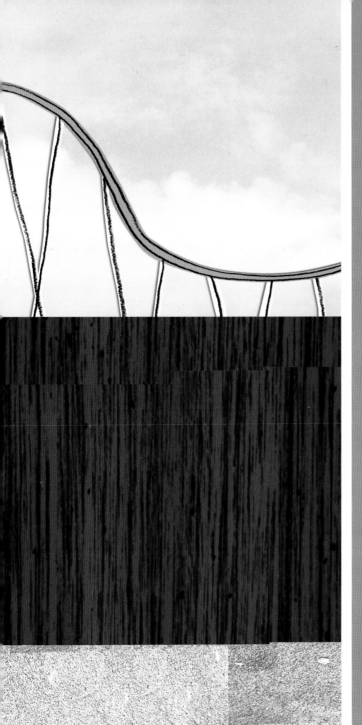

When we get
to the front of the line
Marv says,
"Hold on to your
tummy, Lola!"

But Lola says,
"Err... I think
I might be slightly
too small still.

Perhaps it would be
a little more fun
if I went on something
for more slightly
smaller people –
like the
Chug-a-Bugs!"

So we all go on the **Chug-a-Bugs**
and Lola **laughs** and **laughs**.
She says, "You were right, Charlie!
The **Chug-a-Bugs** IS the very best ride
in the whole world and the universe."